Cub's Journey Home

Georgia Graham

A bear busily carves out the earth
under the roots of a fallen tree.
She drags herself inside, shoves
the mulch against the opening,
and flops down in the darkness.
Through the winter, she will not
eat or drink and no waste will leave
her body.

Outside, in the world she has now forgotten, flakes of snow silently zigzag down. The bear is plump from the autumn harvest. Her coat is full and sleek.

A tiny speck has been lying deep in her belly since the last ice turned to running water and the spring meadows sprang with tender shoots. It remained there when the summer days grew long and hot. And when a chill returned to the air and the leaves became brittle, it waited still. But as the bear falls into a deep winter slumber, the tiny speck begins to grow.

From moon to moon, winter pounds at the world outside. But in the den, all is quiet.

Then, a shrill cry slices through the den. Mother Bear lifts a heavy eyelid. A tiny cub, smaller than his mother's paw, hoists his body forward, dragging his back legs. His fur is wiry and sparse. His eyes are sealed shut and his ears are pinned flat to his head.

As Mother's milk nourishes him and her warm fur surrounds him, he grows.

After as many days as Cub has toes, his eyes open and his ears pop up like half moons. He does not know about the world outside, or winter, or the passing seasons.

Before long, needles of sunlight stab through the entrance of the den. Mother is thin.

Little Cub is restless. Mother pushes through a curtain of lacy ice and crisscrossed twigs and leads them out of the den. Little Cub follows her into the startling light. A breeze runs its icy fingers through his fur.

Little Cub tags behind Mother as she searches for roots, tender shoots, and lush buds. Soon they wander too far from the den to ever go back. Little Cub begins to forget the small world of the winter den. His home is wherever Mother Bear goes.

Little Cub skedaddles up to a tree to climb it. But instead, he smacks into it clumsily. He starts again, pushing upward with his back claws and hanging on with his front paws.

Mother grunts with excitement. He inches higher and higher, then shimmies down again.

Soon the aspen groves are covered with a canopy of green. Every day the sun shines longer and grows warmer on Mother Bear and Little Cub.

Mother swipes at a log with her huge paw,
flipping it over in front of Little Cub. The
pulpy underside is alive with scurrying ants and squiggling
termites. Mother scoops them up with her wide tongue.
Little Cub sniffs, sucking the insects up his nose. He
sneezes and wipes his nose in the grass.

Mother claws at a hole in another log.
Inside there are combs filled with golden
honey. Mother and Little Cub guzzle the sweet
honey while angry bees buzz and sting them. It's a
small price to pay for such nectar.

A flash of spotted brown fur springs up from the tall grass. Mother Bear tears after it.

Little Cub hurries after her. A terrified fawn springs over boulders and logs, then leaps over a creek and out of sight.

Finally, the sun sets on a long day. Mother carves a day bed in a ditch. She nudges Little Cub in and curls around him. Little Cub drifts off, content in this new home.

The countryside explodes into glorious summer. Scattered throughout the forest are sunny meadows, a picnic paradise. Little Cub scrambles to keep up with Mother Bear as she strips branches of their plump ripe berries and gobbles bunches of flowers and grass.

Suddenly, Mother jerks to a stop and sniffs the air.

The air grows heavy and dark. Mother and Little Cub dash one way and then the other.

But they can't escape the smoke. It hurts to breathe. Their eyes sting. Angry orange flames shoot out from every direction and lick at their heels. Little Cub wiggles under a pile of logs and onto a marshy river bank. He plunges into a cool stream and paddles away from the choking smoke.

From a small island, Little Cub watches the flames shoot higher than the moon. A dark blanket rises up and steals the stars from the sky. He shivers and waits.

By morning the flames die out. A dull sun strains to shine behind a gray haze.

Little Cub swims back to the river bank. He has lost his mother.

Little Cub climbs onto a shore of smoldering black sticks. He wails a mournful cry. He wanders everywhere searching for Mother Bear. His shrieks become weak and raspy. There is nothing to eat amongst the charred logs.

But then he catches a new smell that is carried in the breeze.

Little Cub wanders up to the edge of a pit in the ground. It is overflowing with shiny bags of smelly rot.

Several bears are tearing at the bags and lapping up the yummy ooze. *Grrrrr!* A bear, bigger than Mother, is suddenly charging toward him. Little Cub runs in circles, then scurries up a tree, higher and higher. Big Bear shakes the trunk as he starts to climb. But he can't resist the feast below and backs down. He lumbers back to the bags and rummages in the pit with the other bears. Little Cub holds tight. The big bears continue feasting as the day wears on.

Then, quick as a flash, the big bears scatter all at once. Little Cub sways in the tree above the silent dump.

He hears something moving steadily through the bags. A wolverine, not much bigger than Little Cub, lifts his head, sniffs, and continues scavenging. Wolverine is neck deep in treats. He doesn't care about Little Cub up in the tree. When the sun has fallen low, Wolverine finally waddles away. Little Cub waits. Then his stubby legs shake as he inches down the long trunk.

It is dusk. The smoke has lifted now, and the moon rests above the tree tops.

Mother Bear is looking for her cub. Over the crest of a hill and across a ravine, she breathes deeply. Then she drops to all fours and starts walking, following a faint scent. Her pace quickens. Then she breaks into a run.

Exhausted, Little Cub staggers by himself to a hollow in a hillside. He digs into the earth just as Mother Bear once showed him, and closes his eyes. He is lost without his mother.

Suddenly, he wakes up. There are sounds close by.

Suddenly, Mother Bear is beside him. She is licking his forehead.

Mother Bear is home. Little Cub is home.

Dedicated to the Discovery Wildlife Park, Innisfail, Alberta

Published in Canada by Red Deer Press
195 Allstate Parkway, Markham, ON, L3R 4T8
Published in the United States by Red Deer Press
311 Washington Street, Brighton, Massachusetts, 02135

www.reddeerpress.com

We acknowledge with thanks the Canada Council for the Arts, and the Ontario Arts Council for their support of our publishing program. We acknowledge the financial support of the Government of Canada through the Canada Book Fund (CBF) for our publishing activities.

Graham, Georgia, 1959-, author
Cub's journey home / Georgia Graham.
ISBN 978-0-88995-516-5 (bound)
I. Title.

PS8563.R33C83 2015   jC813'.54   C2014-907294-5

Publisher Cataloging-in-Publication Data (U.S)
ISBN 978-0-88995-516-5
Data available on file

Design by Kerry Plumley
Cover illustration by Georgia Graham

Printed and bound in China
5 4 3 2 1